Phin's Adventures
Chunky Cheddar's Big Fall
Scott Kitlarz

In Loving Memory
Linda C. Simonis
1950-2015

"Great is Thy Faithfulness"
Lamentations 3:23

Chunky Cheddar was a fat rat who loved eating more than anything else. He loved eating so much that the moment he saw poor unsuspecting Phin, he immediately hatched a great plan that involved our fishy friend.

Phin was saddened by the events of being flushed down the toilet. He was away from his loving family, lost, alone and in great need of his fishy pack!

Phin immediately began searching for a way out of this smelly situation only to come to a locked gate. Phin continued searching for a way out, with no luck. He only managed to wind up back to where he'd first entered the sewer.

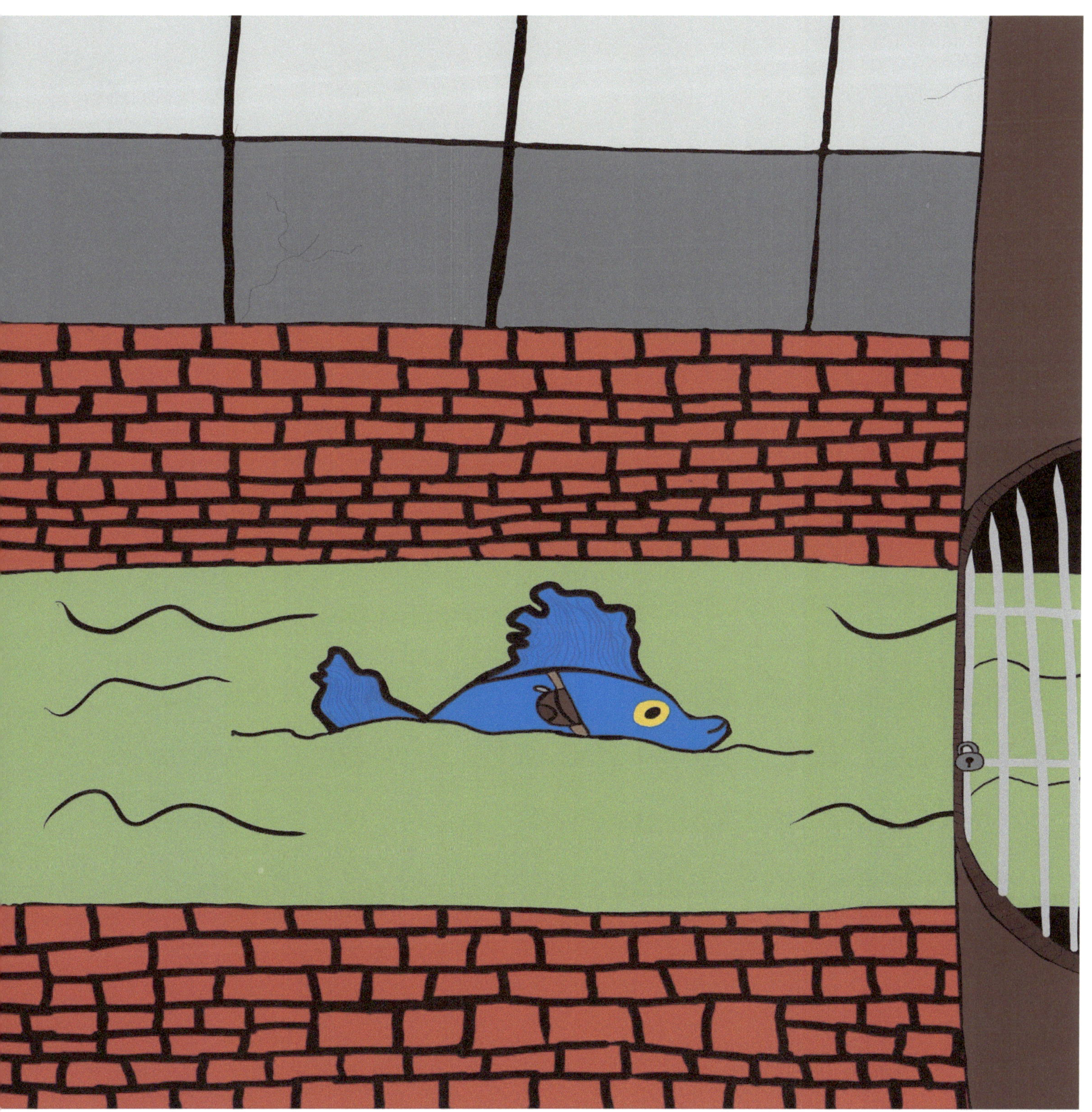

Chunky Cheddar watched with amusement at little Phin's peril. "Looking for your way out?" the fat rat asked, chuckling. Yes," said Phin, looking to the voice above.

Chunky Cheddar smiled, "I have this key that will let you leave the sewers through the locked gates ahead, but first I need your help with something." said Chunky Cheddar

"What is it you need me to do for?" asked Phin. "There are some tasty treats around here, that I saw float by awhile ago!" Chunky Cheddar exclaimed with excitement.

Phin began searching for the treats Chunky Cheddar asked for. After some scouting Phin managed to locate a half bag of soggy potato chips, a surprisingly intact wedge of cheese and a rather suspicious looking piece of pizza.

He swam back to Cheddar, and Phin threw the items of food onto the ledge one by one where the rat sat.

"Thanks, but I think I'm going to have to say no to our trade, get lost!! " said Cheddar.

Before Phin could reply on how unfair Chunky Cheddar was being, he scurried into the shadows of his ledge and began to chomp loudly on his food.

Potato
Chips

Suddenly, there was a loud cracking noise as the ledge upon which Cheddar was lying began to crumble. Years of eating mostly junk food made him so heavy his ledge finally gave way and crumbled beneath him.

Cheddar dropped like a brick into the swirling water below.

Phin watched the whole thing from the key falling from around the giant rats neck into the murky waters around him to the big splash that came after.

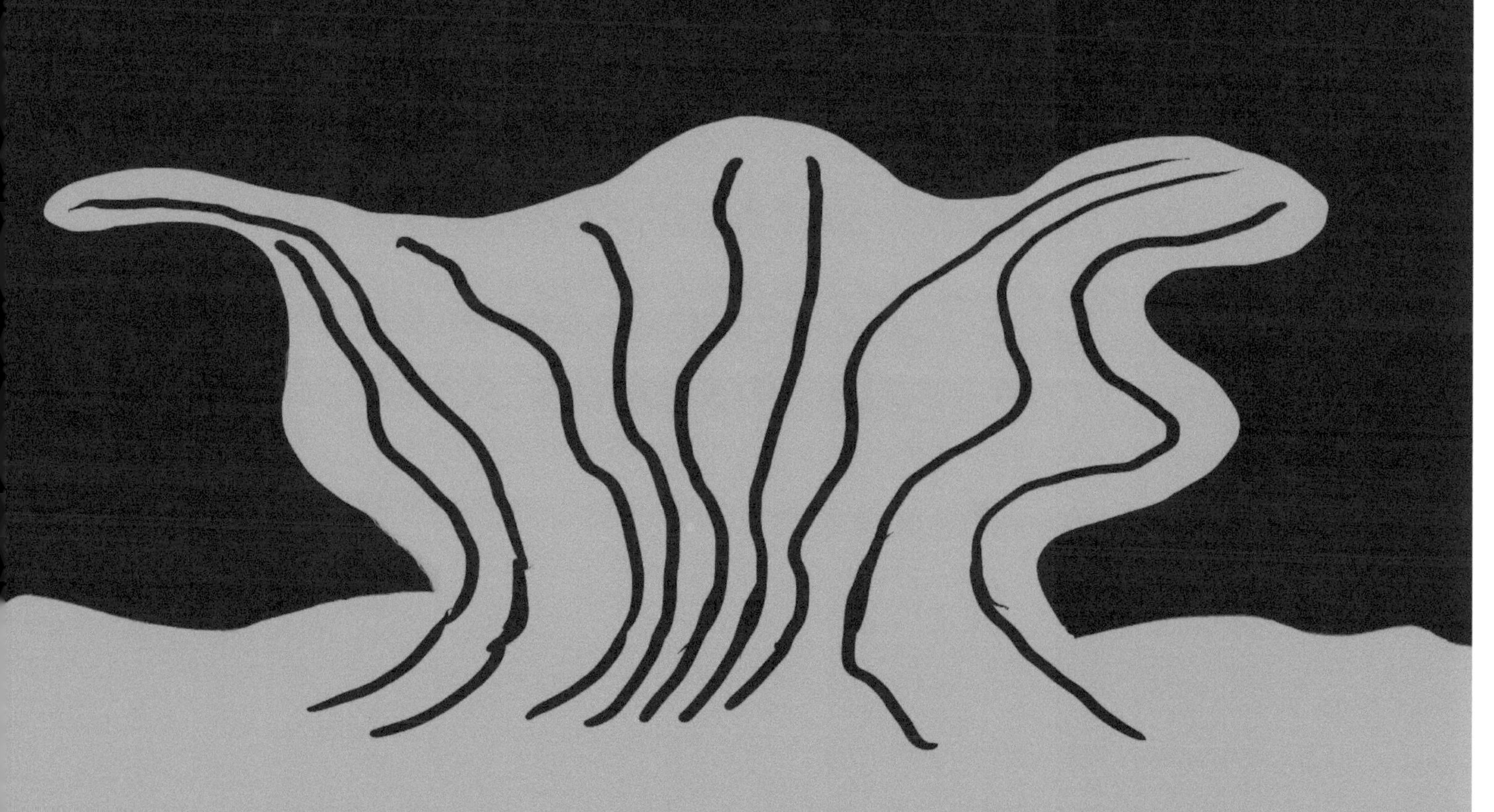

After the waters settled, Cheddar was seen floating on his back. "Help me!!!" The rat cried frantically his paws scratching at the air.

"I will help you but no tricks." said Phin. The brave fish dove under the murky waters looking for the key and while down below not only did he find the key but his fishy pack as well.

Upon surfacing Phin knew better than to hand over the key. He hid the key in his pack and struggled and heaved until Chunky Cheddar was turned right side up. Cheddar swam quickly to sewer ledge and climbed out with great difficulty.

Phin shook his head and said. "You really should try to eat more healthy and exercise once in awhile."

Cheddar rolled his beady eyes and quipped, "Yea, thanks for your help little fish. Take the key and go."

Phin travelled further through the tunnel's sewer and came to the locked gate he had seen earlier. He unlocked the gate and swam through.

As he swam out the exit he saw daylight and what looked like buildings. "I made it." Phin said relieved. In the sky at a distance he saw an object heading towards him.

It was a pigeon, it landed on an old log floating by. As quick as Phin could blink, the pigeon swooped in and picked Phin up by the straps of his fishy pack and was suddenly air-born. "Oh FISH STICKS!!!!" yelled Phin as he was carried off into the unknown.

Join us next time for another of phin's adventures.

Angry Pigeons

Scott Kitlarz is an author from Iowa, he travels with his wife and son from state to state while she is on assignment. Scott has enjoyed reading since he was very young, and his idea for a children's book came to him from a Betta fish he bought his wife as a gift. She named the Betta Phin. Phin traveled with them from state to state and had been on many adventures with his family for about three years before passing away last year. Ultimately Phin was Scott's inspiration to write a series of books about him and what it would be like if he actually were able to go on his own adventures.. Scott has started on his next book for Phin's Adventures and also has other titles in the works.

www.ingramcontent.com/pod-product-compliance
Lightning Source LLC
Chambersburg PA
CBHW042128030726
47599CB00002B/387